Heag̶   ̶o̶
Mvsterv

Chapter 1

I don't know anyone else with a gran like mine. For one thing, she rides an enormous motorbike. It's a BSA Road Rocket and it's jet black with orange flames painted down the sides. It goes like stink. Gran calls it "Fenella" and we hear them coming a mile off. Gran lives in the house over the road from mine where she keeps the bike chained up in her front garden. Gran has a leather jacket with a hedgehog painted on the back. She wears lots of silver rings and her hair's dyed red. But she's not scary; she's anything but. Gran's the softest old bird ever. She's part of a gang called the "Hedgehogs". They're all women and they all ride powerful motorbikes. They're also all over 50.

Mum shakes her head in despair when she hears Gran roaring down the street. "Sixty-two year old grandmothers shouldn't ride motorbikes," she says. Mum's like that. She's full of shoulds and shouldn'ts, dos and don'ts. She can be a right pain. Gran says it's because she loves us so much, she's only trying to look after us. But I get annoyed with Mum sometimes. She thinks the whole world's a big, scary, dangerous place where everyone and everything's out to get you. And one day, horribly, she turns out to be right.

3

Every day, after school, me and my brother Morris go to Gran's. She gives us our tea and looks after us until Mum comes home from work.

I follow Morris through Gran's front gate. My brother's nine – one year younger than me. He likes making cakes, sleeping and watching telly. He's big for his age, and calmer than me.

I take my key out of my purse and let us in.

"I'm in the living room," calls Gran.

Morris and I kick off our school shoes and close the door. He heads straight for the kitchen and I find Gran in the front room. She's standing on her head on a bright pink cushion.

"You need to straighten your legs," I say. I'm interested from a professional capacity. I like gymnastics and I'm in the town junior squad.

"This is Yoga," says Gran. "I'm not after a medal."

Morris puts his head round the door. "There's no chocolate cake left," he says. "I only made it yesterday."

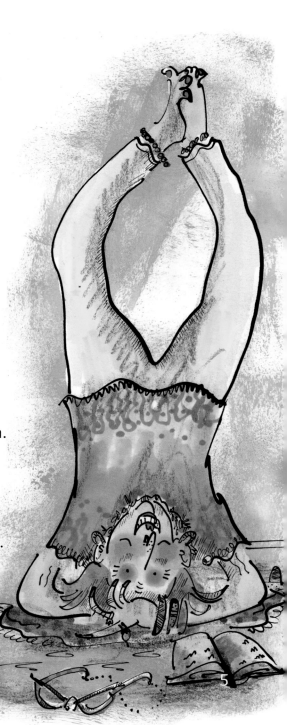

5

"Miss Volpin finished it," Gran puffs through the cushion. She looks funny upside-down. Her cheeks are pink and her eyes bulge. Gran comes down with a thump. "She's only a skinny thing but she eats like a horse," Gran says, sitting up. She looks over my shoulder at the clock. "She'll be back in an hour."

"Who's Miss Volpin?" I ask, returning the pink cushion to the sofa. Gran's very untidy so I help where I can.

Gran grins at me, and the silver glitter on her eyelids twinkles. "My new lodger," she says firmly.

Morris and I groan. "But you SWORE that you'd never have another lodger," I say.

Gran shakes her hair in an annoyed kind of way. "A girl can change her mind, can't she?"

Gran's last lodger was called Delia. She was 19.
She kept losing her door key and flooded the bathroom
three times. She also cried a lot and watched TV really
loud in her room. But what really annoyed Gran was that
Delia had a stinky old rat that kept
escaping and getting into Gran's
bed and weeing. Gran didn't
have the heart to tell Delia
off about it. That's Gran's
greatest downfall; she's as
soft as warm butter. It's one of
the things I love about her.

"Does Mum know?" asks Morris. After Delia, Mum said that she wanted to be at the interview, if Gran was ever, ever going to have another lodger.

"I'm 62 years old," protests Gran, "I can do what I like. And yes she does."

Morris and I exchange looks. Gran sighs and turns to face us. "Fenella's got a base gasket leak and she's blowing oil," she says. "It'll be expensive to fix. Miss Volpin seems charming. She's only in town for two weeks. The money will mend Fenella." Gran glares at us. "I'm not doing without my bike, and you can tell your mother that from me."

"But Gran ..."

"This woman sounds rather fun," continues Gran. "She's a trapeze artist. A performer. She climbs ropes and curtains. You know the sort of thing." We did, but before we can say anything, there's a sharp rap on the door.

"Oh drat," says Gran, leaping up and spilling her tea down her yellow trousers. "It must be Miss Volpin, an hour early."

Chapter 2

Miss Volpin stands in the doorway with two huge suitcases. Maybe she's got her circus things in them? She's so tall she knocks into Gran's chimes. She's wearing tight black trousers, a black jacket and silver trainers. Her dark hair's scraped back into a very tight bun.

"Aren't chimes supposed to go outside?" says Miss Volpin in a sneering sort of voice.

I stiffen. I gave Gran those chimes. They're hung with tiny painted birds and they're always chinking and ringing. It's one of the nice things about Gran's house, that and the smell of motorbike oil.

"You didn't mention there were children living here." The woman shoots an unfriendly look at Morris and me.

"We don't live here," I say, "we live over the road."

Miss Volpin's wearing very strong perfume. It's making my eyes water.

"My daughter's children," says Gran, "and they're no trouble at all." She shoots me a pleading glance.

"All children are trouble," says Miss Volpin. "I'd like to see my room."

Gran picks up the suitcases and insists on heaving them up the stairs.

When they've gone, Morris and I breathe out.

"She's horrible," says Morris.

"She's only here for two weeks," I say, trying to be positive, but even so for the first time ever, Morris and I are relieved when Mum comes to collect us.

Chapter 3

It's Saturday morning and I can sleep for as long as
I like. Or at least, until Gran wakes me up. Every day, at
about eight, Gran goes for a spin on her bike. She says
she'd really like to go at seven but she doesn't want
to wake the neighbours.

I lounge in bed and flick on the radio and listen,
half asleep. The birds are singing loudly in the trees in
the street. It's half past eight now and still no motorbike.

I get out of bed, a pinprick of worry in my stomach. Why hasn't Gran gone out yet?

I part the curtains and look out over the road. Fenella's missing from Gran's front garden. So she's gone out after all. I must have slept through the din. But when I get downstairs, I find Gran in the kitchen. Confusingly, Mum is holding her hand. Morris loafs in the doorway, gloomy-faced.

"Where's Fenella?" I ask.

Gran's still in her nighty and dressing gown. She looks old and haggard. "I'm a stupid old woman," she's saying. "I knew there was something not right."

"Fenella's been stolen," Mum tells me grimly.

"No!" In shock I go over and hug Gran. She feels little and soft and is trying to hide her tears. It's terrible seeing her like this. She's NEVER sad.

"We'll get her back," I say, not having a clue how to do it. "Maybe Miss Volpin saw something?" I hand Gran the screwed-up tissue from my pyjama pocket.

"She's gone too," says Gran in a choked voice.

Chapter 4

The big mystery is that Volpin and the bike vanished without a sound. Gran has already been on the phone to the other Hedgehogs asking if anyone heard a Road Rocket roar early this morning or last night but *nobody* did. Her friend Maggie lives at the crossroads and she's an insomniac. But she heard nothing.

I picture Volpin tiptoeing downstairs in the dead of night and pinching the keys from the hook. She must have wheeled Fenella down the street. It's a dead end so there's only one direction she could have gone.

But why didn't she just ride away?

The policeman arrives at Gran's later that afternoon. He's a big chap with a triple chin and a short beard.

"We probably won't find her," he yawns. "Your Miss Volpin's part of a gang of criminals who make a habit of preying on the elderly." He drains his cup of tea and looks hopefully around for another.

"You should have let me interview her," says Mum. "I wouldn't have let her through the door."

"She's likely to be halfway across the country by now," says the policeman.

Morris and I creep out into the hallway.

"He's not going to help," whispers Morris.

"I know," I reply. "It's down to us." But beyond snooping around Volpin's room for clues (we find none), we're at a bit of a loss.

The policeman leaves and Mum goes off to the shops. Gran can't stay off the phone, ringing round all the local bike shops and traders. But nobody's seen her Road Rocket. Finally she rings off.

"I found out something," she says. "I was just talking to Boris who lives in the next road. He does the fox watch group. He was up at four this morning, watching a vixen, when he saw Miss Volpin walk down the street with her suitcases. He described her exactly, down to her bun and her silver trainers." Gran pauses. "But she didn't have Fenella."

"So maybe it wasn't her who took the bike?" suggests Morris.

But I know Volpin's the thief. She's just done something clever.

"She works in circuses," I say. "She must have made Fenella disappear into thin air."

"Or maybe sawed her in half," says Morris, "and put her in the suitcases."

"Darlings," Gran holds up her hands, "I would have heard if there was any sawing going on." She sighs. "Maybe your Mum's right. I *am* getting too old for all of this."

I look at Gran like she's gone mad. "You don't mean it," I say. "You LOVE biking. You LOVE the Hedgehogs. You said you wanted to bike until you were 80." I can't bear to think of Gran being old and sad, like the frail elderly ladies in the supermarket.

Morris gives me a big nudge and I nudge him back even harder.

"Anyone for another milkshake?" asks Gran. "I think I've got some strawberries left." She goes into the kitchen. Seeing her so sad makes me even more determined to get the bike back.

"You've upset her," whispers Morris.

"No I haven't," I growl. "Miss Volpin did that."

Later, Morris has gone home and Gran's out in the garden doing things to her roses. I think she wants to be on her own but I don't want to leave her. I sit on her pink cushion and try to think. It just doesn't make sense. How could a Road Rocket just vanish into thin air? I look out at the street. It's a lovely sunny afternoon and the birds are chirping away in the big tree outside the house.

I think about Volpin and imagine her swinging from a trapeze and climbing ropes in her silver trainers. A pigeon flaps over the road and lands in the gutter. There's a smear of oil on the pavement that must have come from Fenella. I look at the tree. The leaves are dense and green. I let myself out of the front door. The trail of oil stops at the foot of the trunk, and then appears to travel *up* it.

Automatically, I peer upwards. My mouth falls open.
About 3 metres above, almost completely hidden by leaves,
the trunk splits into two fat arms. From the fattest branch,
suspended by thick ropes, I can see a glint of black metal
and painted flames and the rim of a motorcycle wheel.

Chapter 5

Fenella's up there. All of her! I want to shout for joy. I've found her! Gran can go on the rally after all. I think of her face when I tell her.

But what's the bike doing in the tree? Volpin must

have hauled it up with her ropes. I'm about to dash up to Gran and tell her when I stop myself. Slowly I step back, and it's a very, very hard thing to do. I want to make Gran happy now! But I also have the beginnings of an idea, an idea that'll put Volpin out of business for good.

I find Morris lying on his bed playing music. When I come in, he grins.

"Here's my super-sleuth sister, ready to make her report."

"Turn that music off and listen," I say. When I tell him I've found Fenella, he nearly falls off the bed.

"In the TREE?" he bellows. He rushes to the window. "Where?" I remind him that his window looks over the garden at the back of the house. "Let's go and tell Gran," he says.

But I put out a hand to stop him. "Hold on just a minute," I say. "Let's just think about this." And then I tell him my plan.

I go back round to Gran's to try and cheer her up but the evening just seems to drag on and on. Not telling her about Fenella is the hardest thing I've ever had to do.

Morris has been busy while I was at Gran's. He's charged up Mum's old mobile phone and has copied the police station number, and he's persuaded Mum to lend him her digital camera for an "art project". He's also set up his video recorder in my bedroom window so that it's focused on the tree.

At bedtime, Mum eyes me suspiciously. "What's going on?" she asks. "Why are you being so good? I usually have to ask you a million times to get ready for bed and here you BOTH are in your pyjamas and washed. Something's going on."

She's clever, my mum, I have to hand it to her. "I'm just tired," I say, trying to sound hurt.

In my room, I put my jeans back on over my pyjamas and pull the curtains back a little so I can see the tree from my bed. Luckily, Mum goes to bed early and at half past nine, she comes quietly into my room. I have my eyes shut and I try to breathe deeply and evenly.

"I know you're up to something," she says.

I don't flinch. She waits for what seems like ages and ages but I gut it out. I even do a happy little sleep murmur and turn over in bed. That seems to do the trick because at last she leaves, closing the door quietly. In an instant I'm out of bed and at the window. Outside, the street lights glow in the darkness. When I hear Mum's light clicking off, I put on my big soft, dark jumper and my socks and shoes. Then I get out an apple from my hoard and crunch away, watching and waiting. About half an hour later, Morris creeps in. Like me, he's dressed for the outdoors.

"Seen anything?" he asks softly. I shake my head.

Morris flops on the bed. "Mum's asleep," he says. "I heard her snoring."

"Good," I say. Mum could seriously wreck our plans.

We wait, quietly watching the street. Morris breaks the silence. "Ellie," he says, "how do we know she's going to come tonight?"

"We don't," I reply. "But she's hardly going to leave
it up there for long, is she?"

Morris frowns. "I don't want to wait up all night for
no reason," he says.

"Look," I say. "If she doesn't come tonight, then we'll
tell Gran about the bike. OK? This is our chance to catch
her red-handed."

"All right," Morris agrees reluctantly. After a few
minutes he gets bored of sitting in the window and
stretches out on my bed.

"No going to sleep," I warn him. "We have to respond
as soon as we see her."

Morris yawns. "Why don't we get the police to do this?"
he says, with his eyes closed. "I want to go to sleep."

"Because life isn't like it is on telly," I say. "I bet
the police wouldn't do what we're doing. They'd just get
out a load of forms for Gran to fill in and then cut
the bike down."

"And what is it we're doing?" asks Morris.

"A sting," I say, and feel myself coming alive.
"We're going to nail this horrible woman good and proper."

Half an hour passes and now it's 11 o'clock. I've seen a young couple walk past, holding hands, a man with a dog and a woman out jogging.

Something moves in the shadows of next door's front garden and I hold my breath as a fox tiptoes out into the road and runs down the centre of the street.

By midnight, Morris has gone to sleep and is breathing softly. A silver string of dribble falls on my pillow and I have to resist the urge to shake him awake.

Then I see her. Even though she's some way off, I know it's her. I see her silver trainers glint in the lamplight. And she has a way of walking. She seems to glide over the pavement, straight backed, like she's on wheels. She's moving fast. I'm suddenly filled with panic.

34

35

"Morris, wake up. She's here." I shake him hard
then go back to the window. A horrible thought occurs
to me. What if she cuts down the bike and rides it away
before we've had a chance to do anything? I'd have lost
Fenella after all. It'd all be my fault.

"Morris." He groans and moans and comes to, as I
try to remember the plan.

"Phone the police," says Morris, sitting up.

In my head, I'd imagined calling the police as I saw
her coming. Now she's nearly here and I don't even
know where the phone is.

"Quick," says Morris, in a tired, thick voice, like his throat's full of chips. I grab the phone from my chest of drawers and dial the number as I watch her come closer. She's moving slower now.

"We're going to be too late," whispers Morris, by my side.

The ring tone goes on and on and on. Finally, a recorded voice asks me to listen to the following options. I could scream. She's here. She's standing at the foot of the tree. She's looking all around.

She's looking straight up at me.

Chapter 6

I'm feeling numb as I stare back. Volpin's eyes flash in
the darkness as she gazes up at me, malevolence written
all over her ghostly white face.

"Dial 999," stutters Morris, but it's too late for that.
In a bound, Volpin has landed on the tree, and is
clawing up, like a cat. Now she's out of sight.

"Quick!" I scream. I can't let her get away
with Fenella. Why oh why did I risk it? I half fall down
the stairs and bash into the front door.

"Wrong key," says Morris, fumbling with the lock.

"She's going to get away," I yell, now beyond caring if Mum wakes up. In fact, I want her to wake up. Morris unlocks the door and we spill out into the street.

"Help!" I shout, and my voice echoes around the sleeping houses. I race over the road, my heart thumping.

"It's NOT YOURS!" I shriek up into the leaves. I can't see anything. It's too dark. "Stop her!" I yell at Morris even though it's obvious Volpin isn't going anywhere.

Not yet.

We stand there dumbly, not knowing what to do. I have the mobile in my hand and the recorded voice is still reeling off options.

"I'll do it," says Morris, snatching it out of my hand.

All at once Gran's door flies open and she bursts out in her nighty. "Ellie, Morris, what are you *doing*?" she says crossly. "You'll wake the whole street."

"She's up there," I say hoarsely. "Volpin."

"Up where?" Gran turns to Morris. "Is she sleepwalking? What's going on? Is it a fire?" I cry.

Leaves fall from the tree as the lower branches shake.

"Quick!" I scream. "*She's going to drive it away.*"

"She can't drive it in the air," says Morris reasonably.

"What's up there?" asks Gran, going over to the tree to look.

"Watch out, it might fall on your head," I shout. I know I'm mad and hysterical but I can't stop myself.

"What?" Gran looks thoroughly confused as a twig snaps off and lands by her feet. "Who's up there? Is it a cat?"

"FENELLA!" I scream. "And VOLPIN." I'm breathing fast now.

"It's Fenella!" cries Gran looking up. "She's in the tree. Goodness me."

"So's your lodger," says Morris. "We're trapping her."

The tree goes still and quiet.

"She's planning something," says Morris.

"WHAT DO WE DO?" I cry.

Gran grabs the phone from me and dials a number.
The tree rustles again and I let out a little scream as
a black shadow emerges out of the uppermost foliage and
moves over our heads.

"SHE'S WALKING ON THE TELEPHONE WIRES,"
I yell. I don't seem to be able to speak properly any more.

"SHE'S GETTING AWAY." I stand, open-mouthed, as Volpin balances slowly over the wires above us, her arms outstretched.

When she reaches the middle of the street, the wire's bowing deeply into the road and for a minute I think it's going to break. The wire wobbles.

We hold our breath as she seems to fall but then she's dangling by her hands and pulling herself along. She swings back and forth and lands in the tree outside our house.

Everything goes still.

I'm mesmerised but I manage to pull myself together when a shower of leaves indicates she's on the move again.

"There," shouts Morris.

Volpin has vaulted onto the roof of our house. "You won't catch me," she calls. "Go back to bed." A tile clatters down the roof and smashes on the pavement.

When I look back, Volpin has gone.

"Over there," points Morris and we hurry along the road. Above our heads, Volpin bends and slides and dances over the rooftops, hopping from one house to the next. I have to hand it to her, she's incredible. She's going so fast, like a cross between a monkey and a cat.

"Stop!" shouts Gran way
behind us. "Just let her go."
We pretend not to hear.
I knew Gran would be like
this but I'm not going to lose
Volpin now.

"Thief!" I shout as Volpin
effortlessly leaps up
a steep roof and pit-pats
down the other side.
When we reach the last house
on the street, she stops, dead
still, silhouetted by the moon.
I'm very impressed even
though I hate her. As I watch,
she steps back, then takes
a massive run and leaps into
the void.

"Oh!"

Volpin flies through the air
and lands on a lamppost.
She curls herself around it
and slides to the ground.

Then she runs. Morris and I follow, keeping up as best as we can but we're outclassed.

"WE'RE LOSING HER!" I scream.

Then all at once, the street fills with blinding lights and a massive roar. It's the sound of many big, powerful motorbikes.

The Hedgehogs are coming!

Chapter 7

"Ellie? Morris?" Gran's calling us. I screw my eyes up at the powerful lights.

Gran's riding on the back of Maggie's motorbike. Maggie's wearing a pink towelling dressing gown and bed socks. Behind her there's a convoy of four other bikes, all ridden by old women in night clothes.

"OVER THERE." I point at Volpin sprinting away down the street, way ahead. The Hedgehogs rev their bikes and roar after her.

Betty pulls up beside me. "Come on," she says, handing me a helmet. I barely have time to put it on and climb up behind her before we're off. Behind me, I can see Morris is riding with Alice. I'm glad Mum can't see us. But we're not letting Volpin out of our sight. We catch up with her as we arrive at the crossroads. She takes one look at our convoy and leaps over a low wall into a car park. We burn through the entrance, but Volpin vanishes into the rows of parked cars.

"Circle the car park," I scream, "or she'll get away."
I slip off Betty's bike and run through the cars.

"Ellie, come back," yells Gran, but her voice is
drowned by the motorbike engines.

I lie on the ground, and peer under the nearest car.
Nothing. I wriggle forwards, bruising my knees, to check
the next one; a big saloon. I get the shock of my life when
I see the whites of Volpin's eyes gleaming back at me.

"OVER HERE!" I yell, as she slides away out of sight. She can't get away, she just CAN'T. I stand up as the car park fills with flickering blue lights and watch as Volpin vaults over a Land Rover into the arms of an especially large police officer. She wriggles like anything but he isn't letting her go. In seconds, another police officer clamps handcuffs on her.

We've got her.

As she's marched past me she stops. "I knew you'd be trouble," she hisses. Then she's bundled away into a police car.

The next morning, Mum, Morris and me all gather in the street to watch Gran go off for her ride.

"I thought you were giving up, Gran," I call as she revs Fenella's engine louder and louder.

"Never," she replies, smiling. "Never."

Grannies and grandkids chase midnight bike thief

A woman was arrested shortly after midnight on Saturday. She's held on suspicion of attempting to rob a local grandmother's motorbike, a BSA Road Rocket, known as Fenella.

The grandmother and her beloved bike

The suspect, Miss Volpin, had been lodging with the grandmother and claimed to be a trapeze artist.

Police confirm that she's part of a well-known criminal gang.

The red-haired grandmother 62, a member of the Hedgehogs gang of granny bikers, discovered her bike and Volpin missing on Saturday morning. Fox-watching Boris witnessed Volpin leaving with her suitcases earlier tha morning.

Brave grandkids, Morris and Ellie

The Hedgehogs take chase

Grandchildren Ellie, ten, and Morris, nine, located the bike up the tree in their grandmother's front garden later that day, and planned a sting to nail Volpin.

The suspected bike thief

Shortly after midnight, they witnessed Volpin climbing the tree. Volpin attempted to escape along the telephone wires and house roofs, before sliding down a lamppost. A convoy of the Hedgehogs, joined by Ellie and Morris, roared after Volpin and chased her into a car park, where the police arrested her.

Ideas for guided reading

Learning objectives: compare the usefulness of techniques such as visualisation, prediction, empathy in exploring the meaning of texts; tell a story using notes designed to cue techniques such as repetition, recap and humour; perform a scripted scene making use of dramatic conventions

Curriculum links: Citizenship:

Respect for property

Interest words: hedgehog, professional, gymnastics, downfall, pyjama, insomniac, preying, interview, vixen, red-handed, options, malevolence, foliage, mesmerised, vaulted, silhouetted, saloon, convoy

Resources: writing materials

Getting started

This book can be read over two or more guided reading sessions.

- Invite a child to read the blurb aloud and explain to children that the central character is an unusual grandmother.

- Ask children to close their eyes and imagine words they think describe a grandmother, e.g. *old, kind, wise.* Ask children to describe their own grandmothers, and find out if anyone else has an "unusual" grandmother – do any of the children have a grandmother who owns a motorbike?

- Discuss the description "mystery story". What does a mystery story usually entail?

Reading and responding

- Ask a child to read p2 aloud. Discuss the characters of Gran and Mum, *How are they different?* Discuss how Ellie feels about her gran and her mum.

- Speculate together about what might happen in the story.

- Ask children to read up to Chapter 3 in pairs and discuss the character of Miss Volpin. *Why do you think she isn't very kind? Why is Ellie worried about Miss Volpin living with her gran?*